dead tree
creek

This Rising Moon book belongs to:

Tumbling
boulders

by Marcia Vaughan
Illustrated by Will Terry

the Treasure of Ghostwood Gully

A Southwest Mystery

Rising Moon

www.northlandpub.com

Composed in the United States of America
Printed in China

Edited by Theresa Howell
Designed by Katie Jennings and David Jenney
Production supervised by Donna Boyd

FIRST IMPRESSION 2004
ISBN 0-87358-858-4

04 05 06 07 08   5 4 3 2 1

Library of Congress Cataloging-in-Publication Data

Vaughan, Marcia K.
The treasure of Ghostwood Gully : a Southwest mystery / by Marcia Vaughan ;
illustrated by Will Terry.
p. cm.
Summary: Coyote tries to trick his friends when they set off
to find buried treasure, but Coyote ends up the victim of trickery too.
[1. Coyote—Fiction. 2. Animals—Fiction. 3. Buried treasure—Fiction.]
I. Terry, Will, 1966- ill. II. Title.
PZ7.V452 Tr 2004   [E]—dc22
2004004752

For my son, Sam,
and my husband, Richard,
the real treasures in my life.

—M.V.

To Aaron
and his adventurous spirit.

—W.T.

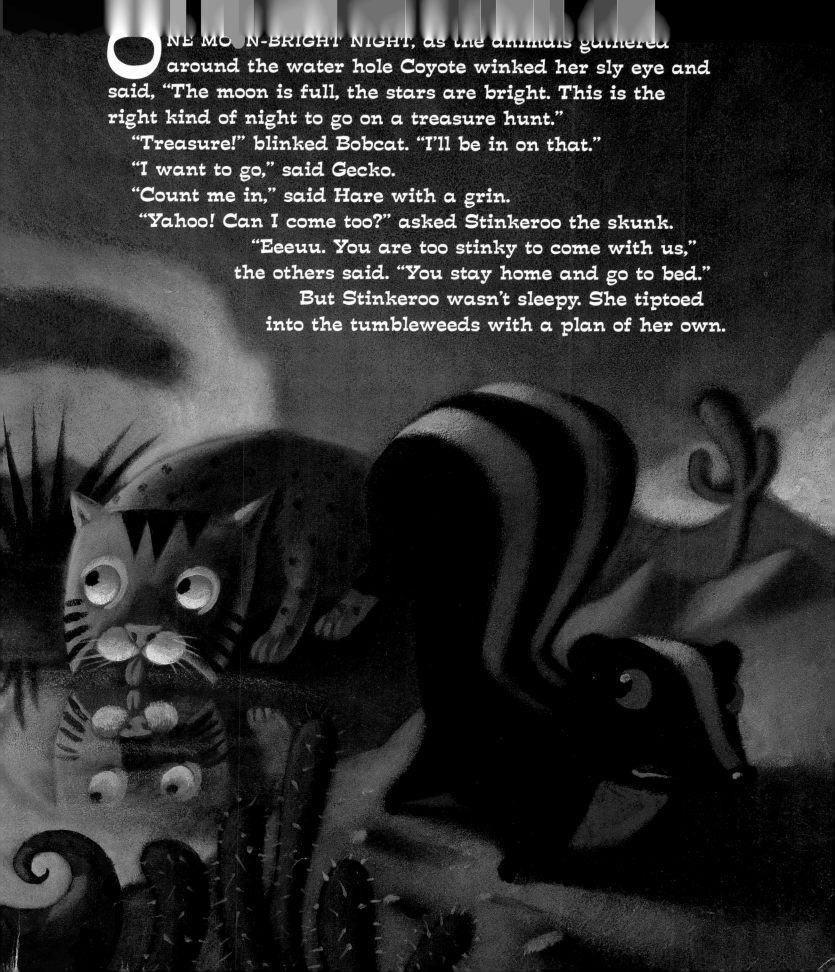

ONE MOON-BRIGHT NIGHT, as the animals gathered around the water hole Coyote winked her sly eye and said, "The moon is full, the stars are bright. This is the right kind of night to go on a treasure hunt."

"Treasure!" blinked Bobcat. "I'll be in on that."

"I want to go," said Gecko.

"Count me in," said Hare with a grin.

"Yahoo! Can I come too?" asked Stinkeroo the skunk.

"Eeeuu. You are too stinky to come with us," the others said. "You stay home and go to bed."

But Stinkeroo wasn't sleepy. She tiptoed into the tumbleweeds with a plan of her own.

Then Coyote said, "I know just the place for you to go. In Ghostwood Gully a chest of treasure can be found, buried deep beneath the ground."

"Let's go find it right now!" the animals cried.

"Beware," Coyote warned. "It won't be easy to reach the treasure. You must go through the Creepy Cave, cross Dead Tree Creek, climb over the tumbling boulders, and pick a spot in the very heart of Ghostwood Gully to dig."

"I don't care," answered Hare.

"I can do that," said Bobcat.

"I'm ready to go," said Gecko.

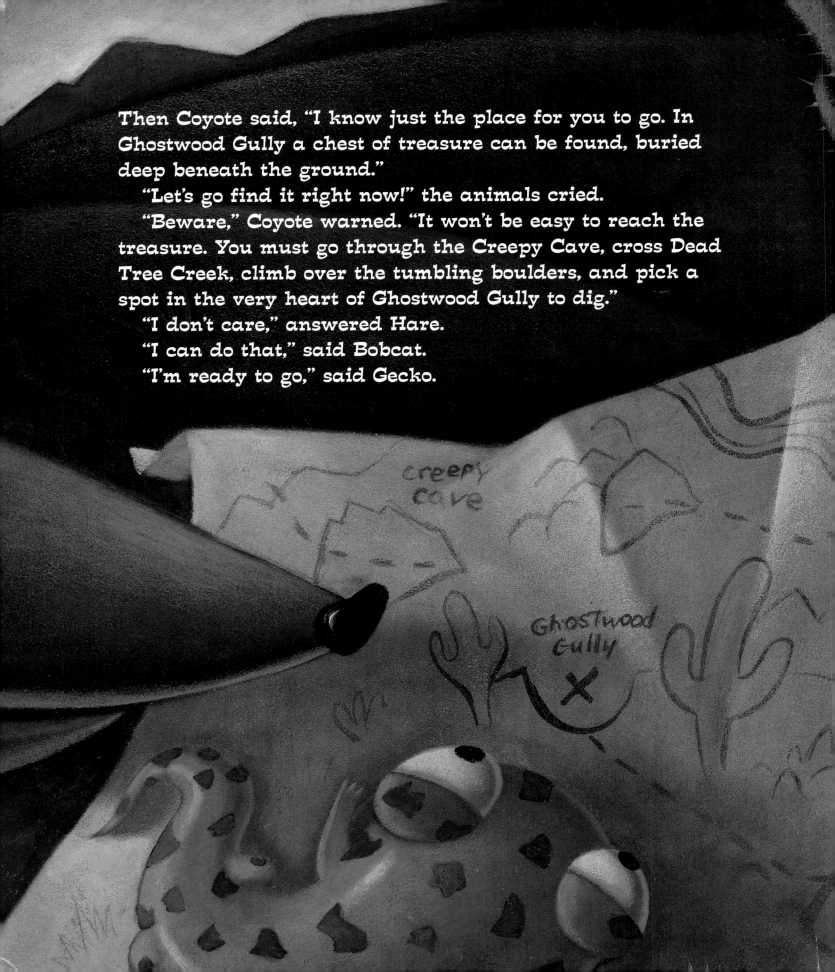

"There's one more thing you must know before you go," Coyote's voice dropped to a whisper. "That long lost hidden loot is still guarded by the ghost of Gus Galoot!"

"Uh-oh," gulped Gecko.

"Imagine that," blinked Bobcat.

"Do we dare?" asked Hare.

But the animals really wanted to go on a treasure hunt.

So quiet as the night, the treasure hunters
marched bravely along until they came to the
mouth of the Creepy Cave. They tiptoed in one
end of the cave as fluttering wings and blinking
things swooped all around them.

"Swish-whish," rustled the grass.

"Ooh-whoooo," wailed the wind.

"BEWARE, TAKE CARE,"
sighed the night.

The treasure hunters had hardly stepped out of the cave when snik-snak, a strange, spooky sound came from the shadows and a voice as cold as ice whispered,

"Stay away!"

"Oh, no," cried Gecko.

"What was that?" blinked Bobcat.

"It gives me a scare," whispered Hare.

But the animals really wanted to find that treasure chest.

So on they hurried through the moonlight until they reached Dead Tree Creek. Bony branches reached out like arms to grab them as they splashed across the muddy creek.

Suddenly, rittle-rattle, a strange spooky sound came from the shadows and a voice as rough as gravel called out,

"Stay away from my treasure!"

"Who's there?" wondered Hare.

"I don't know," gasped Gecko.

"Oh, drat!" snarled Bobcat.

But the animals *really* wanted to find that treasure chest.

So on they trotted until they came to a place where big, black boulders had tumbled across the trail. Step after step, they crept up and over those boulders.

"We're nearly there!" shouted Hare. "Ghostwood Gully is just around the bend."

They rushed through the night, around the bend, and ran smack-dab into a sight that filled them full of shivering fright. . .

"What is that?" cried Bobcat.

"A ghost head to toe," groaned Gecko.

"It's too scary!" said Hare feeling wary.

The animals trembled with fear. But they were so close to finding Gus Galoot's treasure they couldn't turn back.

On they raced. Puffing and panting, they rumbled and bumbled and stumbled along, until...BUMP! They tripped over a shovel. Whip-whap-whomp-wallop! The animals toppled toes over tails into a deep, dark, dirty hole and landed on something hard.

"What is this?" said Bobcat with a hiss.

"I don't know," said Gecko.

"It's hard as a nail," said Hare rubbing his tail.

Beneath them sat a big, brown box with two rusty locks.

"The treasure," the animals cried. "We found the treasure!"

When suddenly, from close by, a voice as dark as midnight cried...

"Who's that sitting on my treasure?"

Oh, the animals were scared stiff. But the treasure hunters really, really wanted to open that treasure chest. They held their breath. Slowly, slowly they lifted up the squeaky creaky lid and peeked inside...

"I GOT YOU!"

"It's the g-g-g-ghost of G-Gus Galoot!"
"Run and hide!" Bobcat cried.
"We better be quick!" said Hare with a kick.
"Let's go, go, go!" called Gecko.

"Wait!
Stop!
Can't you see?
It's only me!"

Coyote tossed back her head with glee.
   "Is that so?" asked Gecko.
   "Good grief," said Hare with relief.
   "I knew that," said Bobcat.
   "You silly animals," Coyote snickered.
"There is nothing to be afraid of. Everybody
knows there is no such thing as a ghost."

But at that very moment Ka-thumpety-bump, a strange, spooky sound came from the shadows and a voice as prickly as cactus cried,

"Boooooo on yoooooou!"

Wearing a tumbleweed suit, out leaped the ghost of Gus Galoot!

"Aaagh!" With a yelp and a shout, Coyote and the animals turned tail and ran. Out of Ghostwood Gully, around the bend, over the big, black boulders, across the creek, under the bony branches, and through the cave. They didn't stop running until they reached the water hole.

As for the ghost of Gus Galoot, she removed her mask and slid slowly out of her tumbleweed suit.

"Going on a midnight treasure hunt," Stinkeroo said, "is much more fun than going to bed."

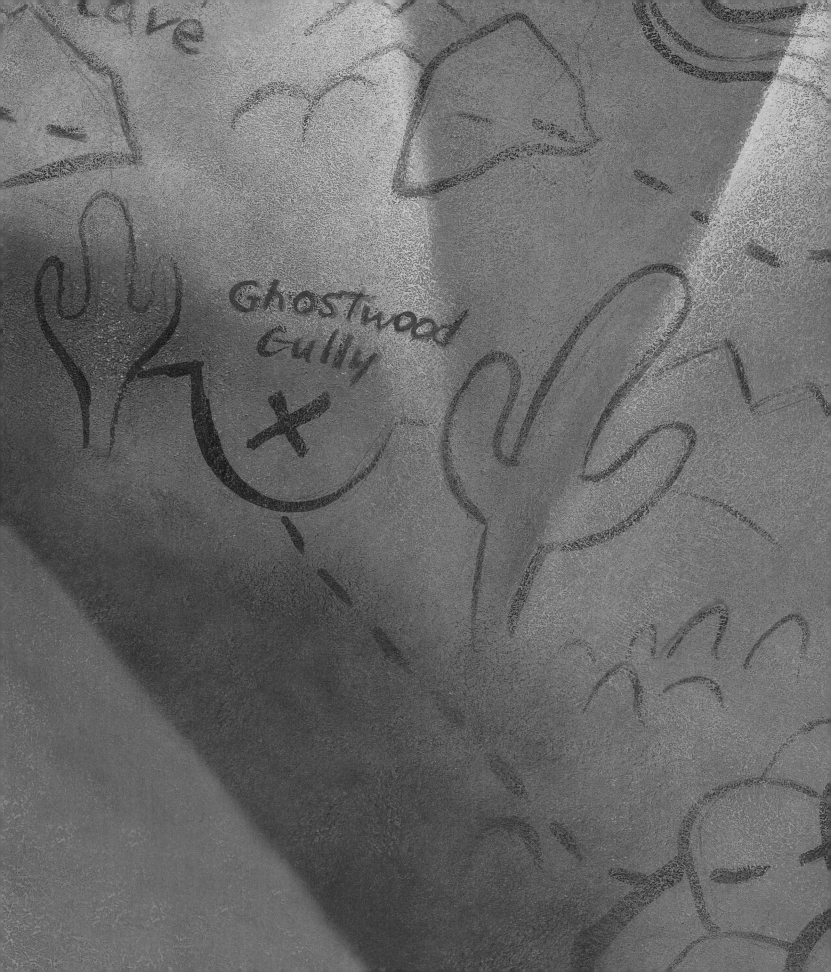